Giles Handley

NO DOUGHNUTS FOR BONKO

Molly Burkett
and
Phil Holland

Molly Burkett
& Bonko

Bonko is a happy fellow. He is short and round and always smiling, well nearly always.

You see, Bonko is a clown and his job is to make people happy, so he is always happy himself, well nearly always.

You wouldn't recognise Bonko when he is ready to go into the ring. He has a bright red nose and bright red cheeks and white rings round his eyes, and he does wear funny clothes. They are much too big for him. His trousers are red and blue checks and he wears a yellow jacket with red lines on it and a bright green collar. If you think that is funny, you should see his shoes. They are a metre long. They are so long that sometimes Bonko trips over them, then he rolls over and over and when he gets up, he's facing quite the wrong way. If his shoes are too big, his hat is too small. It sits on his head like a blue pointed pimple.

Bonko isn't his real name. His real name is Ernest Merryweather but everyone calls him

Bonko. You see, Bonko has a walking stick, but it is a special kind of walking stick. It looks just like an ordinary kind of walking stick but it isn't ordinary at all.

When he is acting the clown in the circus and someone has done something naughty, he says, "I will bonk you on the head." And then he lifts his walking stick in the air and looks as if he really is going to hit them, but, at the last moment, a big, bright green balloon pops out of the end of the stick and Bonko is trying to 'bonk' people with the balloon, and that is something that is almost impossible to do. Bonko is always trying to 'bonk' people in the circus and that is how he came to be called Bonko. After all, it is easier to say Bonko than Ernest Merryweather.

There are two other clowns working in the circus — Tilly and Tally. Those were their real true names. There was Mr. Tally. Everyone called him Tally for short. And there was Mrs. Tally or Matilda Tally, and everyone called her Tilly for short. There were ten little Tallys too, five sets of identical twins. The Tallys were not ordinary clowns like Bonko, they were Pierrots.

They did not wear bright clothes that were too big for them, or shoes that were too long, or a hat that bent in the middle like Bonko's did. They wore smart white suits with ruffs at the necks and wrists and black bobbles down the front. They wore black soft hats on their heads and soft, black shoes on their feet. They looked so smart and so alike that it was difficult to tell which was Tilly and which was Tally.

The Tilly Tallys were very clever. They could turn head over heels. When Bonko tried to turn head over heels he got stuck half way and one of the little Tallys would have to give him a push. The Tilly Tallys could stand on their heads and walk on their hands. Poor Bonko got in such a muddle when he tried. He could stand on one hand and one leg, or

one leg and two hands, or two legs and one hand. He could never get it quite right although the little Tallys kept showing him.

The Tallys could dance and sing and play musical instruments. When Bonko tried to do

all these things, the children laughed. That made Bonko happy. Clowns like people to laugh.

There was a big parade when the circus opened. The ponies came first with plumes on their heads and bells on their harness. Then came the elephants and the dogs and the men from the trapeze and all the other circus folk.

When the parade had finished in came the clowns. Tilly and Tally would be playing a tune on their flutes and skipping round the ring. Then they would fetch a barrel and roll it into the middle of the floor. They would look at it from the top and look at it from the bottom and stand on their heads and look at it from each side. They would shrug their shoulders, pretending the barrel was empty.

They would tie a piece of string to the barrel, strike a match, light the end of the string and run away and cover their ears with their hands pretending to wait for an explosion.

When the flame reaches the barrel, there is a loud shout and out jumps Bonko. He had been in there all the time. He jumps out and runs round and round the ring and everyone shouts. They can see that his trousers have caught fire. Then Tilly and Tally fetch the hosepipe and turn the water on Bonko. The water knocks his hat off and he gets wetter and wetter and he takes the hose and turns it on Tally, then he slips in the water and sits down and the hose gets stuck down his trousers. They do get in a muddle. But one day calamity struck, and it was all Bonko's fault.

BONK

You see, Bonko liked doughnuts. In fact, I think that you could safely say that doughnuts were Bonko's favourite food.

Bonko always liked it when the circus went to Bakerstown because in Bakerstown was the best bakers shop you could ever find. They sold the crustiest loaves and the sweetest cakes and the crispiest tarts, but best of all they sold the biggest, jammiest doughnuts you have ever seen. Bonko liked them so much that he bought ten at a time. He ate doughnuts for breakfast and doughnuts for dinner and doughnuts for tea. By the end of the week. Bonko was beginning to look like a doughnut himself.

Because he was a clown, he always wore clothes that were too big for him, so he didn't notice that he was filling them up a bit more each day — not until he got into the barrel for the show and couldn't get out again.

Tilly and Tally rolled the barrel into the middle of the ring like they always did. They looked at it then they tied the string to it as they did every night and lit it. The flame ran down the string and reached the barrel and

BO

the lid went up, but Bonko did not jump out, in fact, he did not move at all. Instead, he said in a very small voice, “Help.” The audience laughed and laughed. They thought it was part of the show. Tilly and Tally caught hold of Bonko’s arms and pulled and pulled, but he did not budge. He was stuck.

The little Tallys ran into the ring and tried to help. They pulled and pulled. The audience laughed and laughed. But Bonko did not move an inch. He was stuck.

Then Tilly Tally started to sniff. She could smell burning. Bonko’s clothes were on fire. Tilly ran and fetched a bucket of water and tipped it into the barrel. All the little Tallys fetched buckets of water too.

“Help,” said Bonko. “Help, I’m drowning.”

The audience thought it was the funniest thing they had ever seen.

The ringmaster came to see what was happening. He took off his smart black hat when he saw Bonko, and scratched his head.

He didn't know how to get Bonko out of the barrel.

The man who trained the dogs came into the ring, but he did not know how to get Bonko out of the barrel.
Nor did the lion-tamer,
or the trapeze artists,
or the ladies who rode the horses,
or the tight-tope walker,
but the elephant man did.

He brought his two elephants into the ring. He tied a piece of rope to one side of the barrel and the elephant held the other end in his trunk. Then he tied another rope to the other side of the barrel and the other elephant held the end in his trunk.

When he shouted, "Pull," the elephants pulled and the barrel split right down the middle, and there was Bonko looking very sad and very wet and very cold.

Later on when Bonko was wrapped in a blanket and soaking his feet in a mustard

bath, Tilly and Tally and all the little Tallys came to see him.

"You'll have to go on a diet," Tilly told him. "You can have carrots and onions and tomatoes and apples, but you must not eat doughnuts, not for ten whole days. We either have to have a bigger barrel or a thinner Bonko and, as we couldn't push a bigger barrel into the ring, you'll have to become thinner, so no more doughnuts."

"No more doughnuts?" said Bonko sadly.

"No," said Tilly firmly, "not for ten whole days."

Poor Bonko, how could he survive for ten whole days without a single doughnut. Whatever would he do?